THE MAD PLANET

THE MAD PLANET

by Murray Leinster

In All His lifetime of perhaps twenty years, it had never occurred to Burl to wonder what his grandfather had thought about his surroundings. The grandfather had come to an untimely end in a rather unpleasant fashion which Burl remembered vaguely as a succession of screams coming more and more faintly to his ears while he was being carried away at the top speed of which his mother was capable.

Burl had rarely or never thought of the old gentleman since. Surely he had never wondered in the abstract of what his great grandfather thought, and most surely of all, there never entered his head such a purely hypothetical question as the one of what his many-times-great-grandfather—say of the year 1920—would have thought of the scene in which Burl found himself.

He was treading cautiously over a brownish carpet of fungus growth, creeping furtively toward the stream which he knew by the generic title of "water." It was the only water he knew. Towering far above his head, three man-heights high, great toadstools hid the grayish sky from his sight. Clinging to the foot-thick stalks of the toadstools were still other fungi, parasites upon the growth that had once been parasites themselves.

Burl himself was a slender young man wearing a single garment twisted about his waist, made from the wing-fabric of a great moth the members of his tribe had slain as it emerged from its cocoon. His skin was fair, without a trace of sunburn. In all his lifetime he had never seen the sun, though the sky was rarely hidden from view save by the giant fungi which, with monster cabbages, were the only growing things he knew. Clouds usually spread overhead, and when they did not, the perpetual haze made the sun but an indefinitely brighter part of the sky, never a sharply edged ball of fire. Fantastic mosses, misshapen fungus growths, colossal molds and yeasts, were the essential parts of the landscape through which he moved.

Once as he had dodged through the forest of huge toadstools, his shoulder touched a cream-colored stalk, giving the whole fungus a tiny shock. Instantly, from the umbrella-like mass of pulp overhead, a fine and impalpable powder fell upon him like snow. It was the season when the toadstools sent out their spores, or seeds, and they had been dropped upon him at the first sign of disturbance.

Furtive as he was, he paused to brush them from his head and hair. They were deadly poison, as he knew well.

Burl would have been a curious sight to a man of the twentieth century. His skin was pink, like that of a child, and there was but little hair upon his body. Even that on top of his head was soft and downy. His chest was larger than his forefathers' had been, and his ears seemed almost capable of independent movement, to catch threatening sounds from any direction. His eyes, large and blue, possessed pupils which could dilate to extreme size, allowing him to see in almost complete darkness.

He was the result of the thirty thousand years' attempt of the human race to adapt itself to the change that had begun in the latter half of the twentieth century.

At about that time, civilization had been high, and apparently secure. Mankind had reached a permanent agreement among itself, and all men had equal opportunities to education and leisure. Machinery did most of the labor of the world, and men were only required to supervise its operation. All men were well-fed, all men were well-educated, and it seemed that until the end of time the earth would be the abode of a community of comfortable human beings, pursuing their studies and diversions, their illusions and their truths. Peace, quietness, privacy, freedom were universal.

Then, just when men were congratulating themselves that the Golden Age had come again, it was observed that the planet seemed ill at ease. Fissures opened slowly in the crust, and carbonic acid gas—the carbon dioxide of chemists—began to pour out into the atmosphere. That gas had long been known to be present in the air, and was considered necessary to plant life. Most of the plants of the world took the gas and absorbed its carbon into themselves, releasing the oxygen for use again.

Scientists had calculated that a great deal of the earth's increased fertility was due to the larger quantities of carbon dioxide released by the activities of man in burning his coal and petroleum. Because of those views, for some years no great alarm was caused by the continuous exhalation from the world's interior.

Constantly, however, the volume increased. New fissures constantly opened, each one adding a new source of carbon dioxide, and each one pouring into the already laden atmosphere more of the gas—beneficent in small quantities, but as the world learned, deadly in large ones.

The percentage of the heavy, vapor-like gas increased. The whole body of the air became heavier through its admixture. It absorbed more moisture and became more humid. Rainfall increased. Climates grew warmer. Vegetation became more luxuriant—but the air gradually became less exhilarating.

Soon the health of mankind began to be affected. Accustomed through long ages to breathe air rich in oxygen and poor in carbon dioxide, men suffered. Only those who lived on high plateaus or on tall mountaintops remained unaffected. The plants of the earth, though nourished and increasing in size beyond those ever seen before, were unable to dispose of the continually increasing flood of carbon dioxide.

*

By the middle of the twenty-first century it was generally recognized that a new carboniferous period was about to take place, when the earth's atmosphere would be thick and humid, unbreathable by man, when giant grasses and ferns would form the only vegetation.

When the twenty-first century drew to a close the whole human race began to revert to conditions closely approximating savagery. The low-lands were unbearable. Thick jungles of rank growth covered the ground. The air was depressing and enervating. Men could live there, but it was a sickly, fever-ridden existence. The whole population of the earth desired the high lands and as the low country became more unbearable, men forgot their two centuries of peace.

They fought destructively, each for a bit of land where he might live and breathe. Then men began to die, men who had persisted in remaining near sea-level. They could not live in the poisonous air. The danger zone crept up as the earth-fissures tirelessly poured out their steady streams of foul gas. Soon men could not live within five hundred feet of sea level. The low-lands went uncultivated, and became jungles of a thickness comparable only to those of the first carboniferous period.

Then men died of sheer inanition at a thousand feet. The plateaus and mountaintops were crowded with folk struggling for a foothold and food beyond the invisible menace that crept up, and up—

These things did not take place in one year, or in ten. Not in one generation, but in several. Between the time when the chemists of the International Geophysical Institute announced that the proportion of carbon dioxide in the air had increased from .04 per cent to .1 per cent and the time when at sea-level six per cent of the atmosphere was the deadly gas, more than two hundred years intervened.

Coming gradually, as it did, the poisonous effects of the deadly stuff increased with insidious slowness. First the lassitude, then the heaviness of brain, then the weakness of body. Mankind ceased to grow in numbers. After a long period, the race had fallen to a fraction of its former size. There was room in plenty on the mountaintops—but the danger-level continued to creep up.

There was but one solution. The human body would have to inure itself to the poison, or it was doomed to extinction. It finally developed a toleration for the gas that had wiped out race after race and nation after nation, but at a terrible cost. Lungs increased in size to secure the oxygen on which life depended, but the poison, inhaled at every breath, left the few survivors sickly and filled with a perpetual weariness. Their minds lacked the energy to cope with new problems or transmit the knowledge which in one degree or another, they possessed.

And after thirty thousand years, Burl, a direct descendant of the first president of the Universal Republic, crept through a forest of toadstools and fungus growths. He was ignorant of fire, or metals, of the uses of stone and wood. A single garment covered him. His language was a scanty group of a few hundred labial sounds, conveying no abstractions and few concrete things.

He was ignorant of the uses of wood. There was no wood in the scanty territory furtively inhabited by his tribe. With the increase in heat and humidity the trees had begun to die out. Those of northern climes went first, the oaks, the cedars, the maples. Then the pines—the beeches went early—the cypresses, and finally even the forests of the jungles vanished. Only grasses and reeds, bamboos and their kin, were able to flourish in the new, steaming atmosphere. The thick jungles gave place to dense thickets of grasses and ferns, now become treeferns again.

And then the fungi took their place. Flourishing as never before, flourishing on a planet of torrid heat and perpetual miasma, on whose surface the sun never shone directly because of an ever-thickening bank of clouds that hung sullenly overhead, the fungi sprang up. About the dank pools that festered over the surface of the earth, fungus growths began to cluster. Of every imaginable shade and color, of all monstrous forms and malignant purposes, of huge size and flabby volume, they spread over the land.

The grasses and ferns gave place to them. Squat footstools, flaking molds, evil-smelling yeasts, vast mounds of fungi inextricably mingled as to species, but growing, forever growing and exhaling an odor of dark places.

The strange growths now grouped themselves in forests, horrible travesties on the vegetation they had succeeded. They grew and grew with feverish intensity beneath a clouded or a haze-obscured sky, while above them fluttered gigantic butterflies and huge moths, sipping daintily of their corruption.

The insects alone of all the animal world above water, were able to endure the change. They multiplied exceedingly, and enlarged themselves in the thickened air. The solitary vegetation—as distinct from fungus growths—that had survived, was now a degenerate form of the cabbages that had once fed peasants. On those rank, colossal masses of foliage, the stolid grubs and caterpillars ate themselves to maturity, then swung below in strong cocoons to sleep the sleep of metamorphosis from which they emerged to spread their wings and fly.

The tiniest butterflies of former days had increased their span until their gaily colored wings should be described in terms of feet, while the larger emperor moths extended their purple sails to a breadth of yards upon yards. Burl himself would have been dwarfed beneath the overshadowing fabric of their wings.

It was fortunate that they, the largest flying creatures, were harmless or nearly so. Burl's fellow tribesmen sometimes came upon a cocoon just about to open, and waited patiently beside it until the beautiful creature within broke through its matted shell and came out into the sunlight.

Then, before it had gathered energy from the air, and before its wings had swelled to strength and firmness, the tribesmen fell upon it, tearing the filmy, delicate wings from its body and the limbs from its carcass. Then, when it lay helpless before them, they carried away the juicy, meat-filled limbs to be eaten, leaving the still living body to stare helplessly at this strange world through its many faceted eyes, and become a prey to the voracious ants who would soon clamber upon it and carry it away in tiny fragments to their underground city.

*

Not all the insect world was so helpless or so unthreatening. Burl knew of wasps almost the length of his own body who possessed stings that were instantly fatal. To every species of wasp, however, some other insect is predestined prey, and the furtive members of Burl's tribe feared them but little as they sought only the prey to which their instinct led them.

Bees were similarly aloof. They were hard put to it for existence, those bees. Few flowers bloomed, and they were reduced to expedients once considered signs of degeneracy in their race. Bubbling yeasts and fouler things, occasionally the nectarless blooms of the rank, giant cabbages. Burl knew the bees. They droned overhead, nearly as large as he was himself, their bulging eyes gazing at him with abstracted preoccupation. And crickets, and beetles, and spiders—

Burl knew spiders! His grandfather had been the prey of one of the hunting tarantulas, which had leaped with incredible ferocity from his excavated tunnel in the earth. A vertical pit in the ground, two feet in diameter, went down for twenty feet. At the bottom of that lair the black-bellied monster waited for the tiny sounds that would warn him of prey approaching his hiding-place (*Lycosa fasciata*).

Burl's grandfather had been careless, and the terrible shrieks he uttered as the horrible monster darted from the pit and seized him had lingered vaguely in Burl's mind ever since. Burl had seen, too, the monster webs of another species of spider, and watched from a safe distance as the misshapen body of the huge creature sucked the juices from a three-foot cricket that had become entangled in its trap.

Burl had remembered the strange stripes of yellow and black and silver that crossed upon its abdomen (*Epiera fasciata*). He had been fascinated by the struggles of the imprisoned insect, coiled in a hopeless tangle of sticky, gummy ropes the thickness of Burl's finger, cast about its body before the spider made any attempt to approach.

Burl knew these dangers. They were a part of his life. It was his accustomedness to them, and that of his ancestors, that made his existence possible. He was able to evade them; so he survived. A moment of carelessness, an instant's relaxation of his habitual caution, and he would be one with his forebears, forgotten meals of long-dead, inhuman monsters.

Three days before, Burl had crouched behind a bulky, shapeless fungus growth while he watched a furious duel between two huge horned beetles. Their jaws, gaping wide, clicked and clashed upon each other's impenetrable armor. Their legs crashed like so many cymbals as their polished surfaces ground and struck against each other. They were fighting over some particularly attractive bit of carrion.

Burl had watched with all his eyes until a gaping orifice appeared in the armor of the smaller of the two. It uttered a shrill cry, or seemed to cry out. The noise was, actually, the tearing of the horny stuff beneath the victorious jaws of the adversary.

The wounded beetle struggled more and more feebly. At last it collapsed, and the conqueror placidly began to eat the conquered before life was extinct.

Burl waited until the meal was finished, and then approached the scene with caution. An ant—the forerunner of many—was already inspecting the carcass.

Burl usually ignored the ants. They were stupid, short-sighted insects, and not hunters. Save when attacked, they offered no injury. They were scavengers, on the lookout for the dead and dying, but they would fight viciously if their prey were questioned, and they were dangerous opponents. They were from three inches, for the tiny black ants, to a foot for the large termites.

Burl was hasty when he heard the tiny clickings of their limbs as they approached. He seized the sharp-pointed snout of the victim, detached from the body, and fled from the scene.

Later, he inspected his find with curiosity. The smaller victim had been a minotaur beetle, with a sharp-pointed horn like that of a rhinoceros to reinforce his offensive armament, already dangerous because of his wide jaws. The jaws of a beetle work from side to side, instead of up and down, and this had made the protection complete in no less than three directions.

Burl inspected the sharp, dagger-like instrument in his hand. He felt its point, and it pricked his finger. He flung it aside as he crept to the hiding-place of his tribe. There were only twenty of them, four or five men, six or seven women, and the rest girls and children.

Burl had been wondering at the strange feelings that came over him when he looked at one of the girls. She was younger than Burl—perhaps eighteen—and fleeter of foot than he. They talked together, sometimes, and once or twice Burl shared with her an especially succulent find of foodstuffs.

*

The next morning he found the horn where he had thrown it, sticking in the flabby side of a toadstool. He pulled it out, and gradually, far back in his mind, an idea began to take shape. He sat for some time with the thing in his hand, considering it with a far-away look in his eyes. From time to time he stabbed at a toadstool, awkwardly, but with gathering skill. His imagination began to work fitfully. He visualized himself stabbing food with it as the larger beetle had stabbed the former owner of the weapon he had in his hand.

Burl could not imagine himself coping with one of the fighting insects. He could only picture himself, dimly, stabbing something that was food with this death-dealing thing. It was no longer than his arm and though clumsy to the hand, an effective and terribly sharp implement.

He thought: Where was there food, food that lived, that would not fight back? Presently he rose and began to make his way toward the tiny river. Yellow-bellied newts swam in its waters. The swimming larvae of a thousand insects floated about its surface or crawled upon its bottom.

There were deadly things there, too. Giant crayfish snapped their horny claws at the unwary. Mosquitoes of four-inch wing-spread sometimes made their humming way above the river. The last survivors of their race, they were dying out for lack of the plant-juices on which the male of the species lived, but even so they were formidable. Burl had learned to crush them with fragments of fungus.

He crept slowly through the forest of toadstools. Brownish fungus was underfoot. Strange orange, red, and purple molds clustered about the bases of the creamy toadstool stalks. Once Burl paused to run his sharp-pointed weapon through a fleshy stalk and reassure himself that what he planned was practicable.

He made his way furtively through the forest of misshapen growths. Once he heard a tiny clicking, and froze into stillness. It was a troop of four or five ants, each some eight inches long, returning along their habitual pathway to their city. They moved sturdily, heavily laden, along the route marked with the black and odorous formic acid exuded from the bodies of their comrades. Burl waited until they had passed, then went on.

He came to the bank of the river. Green scum covered a great deal of its surface, scum occasionally broken by a slowly enlarging bubble of some gas released from decomposing matter on the bottom. In the center of the placid stream the current ran a little more swiftly, and the water itself was visible.

Over the shining current, water-spiders ran swiftly. They had not shared in the general increase of size that had taken place in the insect world. Depending upon the capillary qualities of the water to support them, an increase in size and weight would have deprived them of the means of locomotion.

From the spot where Burl first peered at the water the green scum spread out for many yards into the stream. He could not see what swam and wriggled and crawled beneath the evil-smelling covering. He peered up and down the banks.

Perhaps a hundred and fifty yards below, the current came near the shore. An outcropping of rock there made a steep descent to the river, from which yellow shelf-fungi stretched out. Dark red and orange above, they were light yellow below, and they formed a series of platforms above the smoothly flowing stream. Burl made his way cautiously toward them.

On his way he saw one of the edible mushrooms that formed so large a part of his diet, and paused to break from the flabby flesh an amount that would feed him for many days. It was too often the custom of his people to find a store of food, carry it to their hiding place, and then gorge themselves for days, eating, sleeping, and waking only to eat again until the food was gone.

Absorbed as he was in his plan of trying his new weapon, Burl was tempted to return with his booty. He would give Saya of this food, and they would eat together. Saya was the maiden who roused unusual emotions in Burl. He felt strange impulses stirring within him when she was near, a desire to touch her, to caress her. He did not understand.

He went on, after hesitating. If he brought her food, Saya would be pleased, but if he brought her of the things that swam in the stream, she would be still more pleased. Degraded as his tribe had become, Burl was yet a little more intelligent than they. He was an atavism, a throwback to ancestors who had cultivated the earth and subjugated its animals. He had a vague idea of pride, unformed but potent.

No man within memory had hunted or slain for food. They knew of meat, yes, but it had been the fragments left by an insect hunter, seized and carried away by the men before the perpetually alert ant colonies had sent their foragers to the scene.

If Burl did what no man before him had done, if he brought a whole carcass to his tribe, they would envy him. They were preoccupied solely with their stomachs, and after that with the preservation of their lives. The perpetuation of the race came third in their consideration.

They were herded together in a leaderless group, coming to the same hiding place that they might share in the finds of the lucky and gather comfort from their numbers. Of weapons, they had none. They sometimes used stones to crack open the limbs of the huge insects they found partly devoured, cracking them open for the sweet meat to be found inside, but they sought safety from their enemies solely in flight and hiding.

Their enemies were not as numerous as might have been imagined. Most of the meat-eating insects have their allotted prey. The sphex—a hunting wasp—feeds solely upon grasshoppers. Others wasps eat flies only. The pirate-bee eats bumblebees only. Spiders were the principal enemies of man, as they devour with a terrifying impartiality all that falls into their clutches.

Burl reached the spot from which he might gaze down into the water. He lay prostrate, staring into the shallow depths. Once a huge crayfish, as long as Burl's body, moved leisurely across his vision. Small fishes and even the huge newts fled before the voracious creature.

After a long time the tide of underwater life resumed its activity. The wriggling grubs of the dragonflies reappeared. Little flecks of silver swam into view—a school of tiny fish. A larger fish appeared, moving slowly through the water.

Burl's eyes glistened and his mouth watered. He reached down with his long weapon. It barely touched the water. Disappointment filled him, yet the nearness and the apparent practicability of his scheme spurred him on.

He considered the situation. There were the shelf-fungi below him. He rose and moved to a point just above them, then thrust his spear down. They resisted its point. Burl felt them tentatively with his foot, then dared to thrust his weight to them. They held him firmly. He clambered down and lay flat upon them, peering over the edge as before.

The large fish, as long as Burl's arm, swam slowly to and fro below him. Burl had seen the former owner of his spear strive to thrust it into his opponents, and knew that a thrust was necessary. He had tried his weapon upon toadstools—had practiced with it. When the fish swam below him, he thrust sharply downward. The spear seemed

16

to bend when it entered the water, and missed its mark by inches, to Burl's astonishment. He tried again and again.

He grew angry with the fish below him for eluding his efforts to kill it. Repeated strokes had left it untouched, and it was unwary, and did not even try to run away.

Burl became furious. The big fish came to rest directly beneath his hand. Burl thrust downward with all his strength. This time the spear, entering vertically, did not seem to bend. It went straight down. Its point penetrated the scales of the swimmer below, transfixing that lazy fish completely.

An uproar began. The fish, struggling to escape, and Burl, trying to draw it up to his perch, made a huge commotion. In his excitement Burl did not observe a tiny ripple some distance away. The monster crayfish was attracted by the disturbance, and was approaching.

The unequal combat continued. Burl hung on desperately to the end of his spear. Then there was a tremor in Burl's support, it gave way, and fell into the stream with a mighty splash. Burl went under, his eyes open, facing death. And as he sank, his wide-open eyes saw waved before him the gaping claws of the huge crayfish, large enough to sever a limb with a single stroke of their jagged jaws.

*

He opened his mouth to scream—a replica of the terrible screams of his grandfather, seized by a black-bellied tarantula years before—but no sound came forth. Only bubbles floated to the surface of the water. He beat the unresisting fluid with his hands—he did not know how to swim. The colossal creature approached leisurely, while Burl struggled helplessly.

His arms struck a solid object, and grasped it convulsively. A second later he had swung it between himself and the huge crustacean. He felt a shock as the mighty jaws closed upon the corklike fungus, then felt himself drawn upward as the crayfish released his hold and the shelf-fungus floated to the surface. Having given way beneath him, it had been carried below him in his fall, only to rise within his reach just when most needed.

Burl's head popped above water and he saw a larger bit of the fungus floating near by. Less securely anchored to the rocks of the river bank than the shelf to which Burl had trusted himself, it had been dislodged when the first shelf gave way. It was larger than the fragment to which Burl clung, and floated higher in the water.

Burl was cool with a terrible self-possession. He seized it and struggled to draw himself on top of it. It tilted as his weight came upon it, and nearly overturned, but he paid no heed. With desperate haste, he clawed with hands and feet until he could draw himself clear of the water, of which he would forever retain a slight fear.

As he pulled himself upon the furry, orange-brown upper surface, a sharp blow struck his foot. The crayfish, disgusted at finding only what was to it a tasteless morsel in the shelf-fungus, had made a languid stroke at Burl's wriggling foot in the water. Failing to grasp the fleshy member, the crayfish retreated, disgruntled and annoyed.

And Burl floated downstream, perched, weaponless and alone, frightened and in constant danger, upon a flimsy raft composed of a degenerate fungus floating soggily in the water. He floated slowly down the stream of a river in whose waters death lurked unseen, upon whose banks was peril, and above whose reaches danger fluttered on golden wings.

It was a long time before he recovered his self-possession, and when he did he looked first for his spear. It was floating in the water, still transfixing the fish whose capture had endangered Burl's life. The fish now floated with its belly upward, all life gone.

So insistent was Burl's instinct for food that his predicament was forgotten when he saw his prey just out of his reach. He gazed at it, and his mouth watered, while his cranky craft went downstream, spinning slowly in the current. He lay flat on the floating fungoid, and strove to reach out and grasp the end of the spear.

The raft tilted and nearly flung him overboard again. A little later he discovered that it sank more readily on one side than on the other. That was due, of course, to the greater thickness—and consequently greater buoyancy—of the part which had grown next the rocks of the river bank.

Burl found that if he lay with his head stretching above that side, it did not sink into the water. He wriggled into this new position, then, and waited until the slow revolution of his vessel brought the spear-shaft near him. He stretched his fingers and his arm, and touched, then grasped it.

A moment later he was tearing strips of flesh from the side of the fish and cramming the oily mess into his mouth with great enjoyment. He had lost his edible mushroom. That danced upon the waves several yards away, but Burl ate contentedly of what he possessed. He did not worry about what was before him. That lay in the future, but suddenly he realized that he was being carried farther and farther from Saya, the maiden of his tribe who caused strange bliss to steal over him when he contemplated her.

The thought came to him when he visualized the delight with which she would receive a gift of part of the fish he had caught. He was suddenly stricken with dumb sorrow. He lifted his head and looked longingly at the river banks.

A long, monotonous row of strangely colored fungus growths. No healthy green, but pallid, cream-colored toadstools, some bright orange, lavender, and purple molds, vivid carmine "rusts" and mildews, spreading up the banks from the turgid slime. The sun was not a ball of fire, but merely shone as a bright golden patch in the haze-filled sky, a patch whose limits could not be defined or marked.

In the faintly pinkish light that filtered down through the air, a multitude of flying objects could be seen. Now and then a cricket or a grasshopper made its bullet-like flight from one spot to another. Huge butterflies fluttered gayly above the silent, seemingly lifeless world. Bees lumbered anxiously about, seeking the cross-shaped flowers of the monster cabbages. Now and then a slender-waisted, yellow-stomached wasp flew alertly through the air.

Burl watched them with a strange indifference. The wasps were as long as he himself. The bees, on end, could match his height. The butterflies ranged from tiny creatures barely capable of shading his face to colossal things in the folds of whose wings he could have been lost. And above him fluttered dragonflies, whose long, spindle-like bodies were three times the length of his own.

Burl ignored them all. Sitting there, an incongruous creature of pink skin and soft brown hair upon an orange fungus floating in midstream, he was filled with despondency because the current carried him forever farther and farther from a certain slender-limbed maiden of his tiny tribe, whose glances caused an odd commotion in his breast.

*

The day went on. Once, Burl saw upon the blue-green mold that spread upward from the river, a band of large, red Amazon ants, marching in orderly array, to raid the city of a colony of black ants, and carry away the eggs they would find there. The eggs would be hatched, and the small black creatures made the slaves of the brigands who had stolen them.

The Amazon ants can live only by the labor of their slaves, and for that reason are mighty warriors in their world. Later, etched against the steaming mist that overhung everything as far as the eye could reach, Burl saw strangely shaped, swollen branches rearing themselves from the ground. He knew what they were. A hard-rinded fungus that grew upon itself in peculiar mockery of the vegetation that had vanished from the earth.

And again he saw pear-shaped objects above some of which floated little clouds of smoke. They, too, were fungus growths, puffballs, which when touched emit what seems a puff of vapor. These would have towered above Burl's head, had he stood beside them.

And then, as the day drew to an end, he saw in the distance what seemed a range of purple hills. They were tall hills to Burl, some sixty or seventy feet high, and they seemed to be the agglomeration of a formless growth, multiplying its organisms and forms upon itself until the whole formed an irregular, cone-shaped mound. Burl watched them apathetically.

Presently, he ate again of the oily fish. The taste was pleasant to him, accustomed to feed mostly upon insipid mushrooms. He stuffed himself, though the size of his prey left by far the larger part uneaten.

He still held his spear firmly beside him.

It had brought him into trouble, but Burl possessed a fund of obstinacy. Unlike most of his tribe, he associated the spear with the food it had secured, rather than the difficulty into which it had led him. When he had eaten his fill he picked it up and examined it again. The sharpness of its point was unimpaired.

Burl handled it meditatively, debating whether or not to attempt to fish again. The shakiness of his little raft dissuaded him, and he abandoned the idea. Presently he stripped a sinew from the garment about his middle and hung the fish about his neck with it. That would leave him both hands free. Then he sat cross-legged upon the soggily floating fungus, like a pink-skinned Buddha, and watched the shores go by.

Time had passed, and it was drawing near sunset. Burl, never having seen the sun save as a bright spot in the overhanging haze, did not think of the coming of night as "sunset." To him it was the letting down of darkness from the sky.

Today happened to be an exceptionally bright day, and the haze was not as thick as usual. Far to the west, the thick mist turned to gold, while the thicker clouds above became blurred masses of dull red. Their shadows seemed like lavender, from the contrast of shades. Upon the still surface of the river, all the myriad tints and shadings were reflected with an incredible faithfulness, and the shining tops of the giant mushrooms by the river brim glowed faintly pink.

THE MAD PLANET

Dragonflies buzzed over his head in their swift and angular flight, the metallic luster of their bodies glistening in the rosy light. Great yellow butterflies flew lightly above the stream. Here, there, and everywhere upon the water appeared the shell-formed boats of a thousand caddis flies, floating upon the surface while they might.

Burl could have thrust his hand down into their cavities and seized the white worms that inhabited the strange craft. The huge bulk of a tardy bee droned heavily overhead. Burl glanced upward and saw the long proboscis and the hairy hinder legs with their scanty load of pollen. He saw the great, multiple-lensed eyes with their expression of stupid preoccupation, and even the sting that would mean death alike for him and for the giant insect, should it be used.

The crimson radiance grew dim at the edge of the world. The purple hills had long been left behind. Now the slender stalks of ten thousand round-domed mushrooms lined the river bank and beneath them spread fungi of all colors, from the rawest red to palest blue, but all now fading slowly to a monochromatic background in the growing dusk.

The buzzing, fluttering, and the flapping of the insects of the day died slowly down, while from a million hiding places there crept out into the deep night soft and furry bodies of great moths, who preened themselves and smoothed their feathery antennae before taking to the air. The strong-limbed crickets set up their thunderous noise—grown gravely bass with the increasing size of the organs by which the sound was made—and then there began to gather on the water those slender spirals of tenuous mist that would presently blanket the stream in a mantle of thin fog.

*

Night fell. The clouds above seemed to lower and grow dark. Gradually, now a drop and then a drop, now a drop and then a drop, the languid fall of large, warm raindrops that would drip from the moisture-laden skies all through the night began. The edge of the stream became a place where great disks of coolly glowing flame appeared.

The mushrooms that bordered on the river were faintly phosphorescent (*Pleurotus phosphoreus*) and shone coldly upon the "rusts" and flake-fungi beneath their feet. Here and there a ball of lambent flame appeared, drifting idly above the steaming, festering earth.

Thirty thousand years before, men had called them "will-o'-the-wisps," but Burl simply stared at them, accepting them as he accepted all that passed. Only a man attempting to advance in the scale of civilization tries to explain everything that he sees. The savage and the child is most often content to observe without comment, unless he repeats the legends told him by wise folk who are possessed by the itch of knowledge.

Burl watched for a long time. Great fireflies whose beacons lighted up their surroundings for many yards—fireflies Burl knew to be as long as his spear—shed their intermittent glows upon the stream. Softly fluttering wings, in great beats that poured torrents of air upon him, passed above Burl.

The air was full of winged creatures. The night was broken by their cries, by the sound of their invisible wings, by their cries of anguish and their mating calls. Above him and on all sides the persistent, intense life of the insect world went on ceaselessly, but Burl rocked back and forth upon his frail mushroom boat and wished to weep because he was being carried from his tribe, and from Saya—Saya of the swift feet and white teeth, of the shy smile.

Burl may have been homesick, but his principal thoughts were of Saya. He had dared greatly to bring a gift of fresh meat to her, meat captured as meat had never been known to be taken by a member of the tribe. And now he was being carried from her!

He lay, disconsolate, upon his floating atom on the water for a great part of the night. It was long after midnight when the mushroom raft struck gently and remained grounded upon a shallow in the stream.

23

THE MAD PLANET

When the light came in the morning, Burl gazed about him keenly. He was some twenty yards from the shore, and the greenish scum surrounded his now disintegrating vessel. The river had widened out until the other bank was barely to be seen through the haze above the surface of the river, but the nearer shore seemed firm and no more full of dangers than the territory his tribe inhabited. He felt the depth of the water with his spear, then was struck with the multiple usefulness of that weapon. The water would come to but slightly above his ankles.

Shivering a little with fear, Burl stepped down into the water, then made for the bank at the top of his speed. He felt a soft something clinging to one of his bare feet. With an access of terror, he ran faster, and stumbled upon the shore in a panic. He stared down at his foot. A shapeless, flesh-colored pad clung to his heel, and as Burl watched, it began to swell slowly, while the pink of its wrinkled folds deepened.

It was no more than a leech, sharing in the enlargement nearly all the lower world had undergone, but Burl did not know that. He thrust at it with the side of his spear, then scraped frantically at it, and it fell off, leaving a blotch of blood upon the skin where it came away. It lay, writhing and pulsating, upon the ground, and Burl fled from it.

He found himself in one of the toadstool forests with which he was familiar, and finally paused, disconsolately. He knew the nature of the fungus growths about him, and presently fell to eating. In Burl the sight of food always produced hunger—a wise provision of nature to make up for the instinct to store food, which he lacked.

Burl's heart was small within him. He was far from his tribe, and far from Saya. In the parlance of this day, it is probable that no more than forty miles separated them, but Burl did not think of distances. He had come down the river. He was in a land he had never known or seen. And he was alone.

All about him was food. All the mushrooms that surrounded him were edible, and formed a store of sustenance Burl's whole tribe could not have eaten in many days, but that very fact brought Saya to his mind more forcibly. He squatted on the ground, wolfing down the insipid mushroom in great gulps, when an idea suddenly came to him with all the force of inspiration.

He would bring Saya here, where there was food, food in great quantities, and she would be pleased. Burl had forgotten the large and oily fish that still hung down his back from the sinew about his neck, but now he rose, and its flapping against him reminded him again.

He took it and fingered it all over, getting his hands and himself thoroughly greasy in the process, but he could eat no more. The thought of Saya's pleasure at the sight of that, too, reinforced his determination.

With all the immediacy of a child or a savage he set off at once. He had come along the bank of the stream. He would retrace his steps along the bank of the stream.

Through the awkward aisles of the mushroom forest he made his way, eyes and ears open for possibilities of danger. Several times he heard the omnipresent clicking of ants on their multifarious businesses in the wood, but he could afford to ignore them. They were short-sighted at best, and at worst they were foragers rather than hunters. He only feared one kind of ant, the army-ant, which sometimes travels in hordes of millions, eating all that it comes upon. In ages past, when they were tiny creatures not an inch long, even the largest animals fled from them. Now that they measured a foot in length, not even the gorged spiders whose distended bellies were a yard in thickness, dared offer them battle.

The mushroom forest came to an end. A cheerful grasshopper (*Ephigger*) munched delicately at some dainty it had found. Its hind legs were bunched beneath it in perpetual readiness for flight. A monster wasp appeared above—as long as Burl himself—poised an instant, dropped, and seized the luckless feaster.

THE MAD PLANET

There was a struggle, then the grasshopper became helpless, and the wasp's flexible abdomen curved delicately. Its sting entered the jointed armor of its prey, just beneath the head. The sting entered with all the deliberate precision of a surgeon's scalpel, and all struggle ceased.

The wasp grasped the paralyzed, not dead, insect and flew away. Burl grunted, and passed on. He had hidden when the wasp darted down from above.

The ground grew rough, and Burl's progress became painful. He clambered arduously up steep slopes and made his way cautiously down their farther sides. Once he had to climb through a tangled mass of mushrooms so closely placed, and so small, that he had to break them apart with blows of his spear before he could pass, when they shed upon him torrents of a fiery red liquid that rolled off his greasy breast and sank into the ground (*Lactarius deliciosus*).

A strange self-confidence now took possession of Burl. He walked less cautiously and more boldly. The mere fact that he had struck something and destroyed it provided him with a curious fictitious courage.

He had climbed slowly to the top of a red clay cliff, perhaps a hundred feet high, slowly eaten away by the river when it overflowed. Burl could see the river. At some past floodtime it had lapped at the base of the cliff on whose edge he walked, though now it came no nearer than a quarter-mile.

The cliffside was almost covered with shelf-fungi, large and small, white, yellow, orange, and green, in indescribable confusion and luxuriance. From a point halfway up the cliff the inch-thick cable of a spider's web stretched down to an anchorage on the ground, and the strangely geometrical pattern of the web glistened evilly.

Somewhere among the fungi of the cliffside the huge creature waited until some unfortunate prey should struggle helplessly in its monster snare. The spider waited in a motionless, implacable patience, invincibly certain of prey, utterly merciless to its victims.

MURRAY LEINSTER

Burl strutted on the edge of the cliff, a silly little pink-skinned creature with an oily fish slung about his neck and a draggled fragment of a moth's wing about his middle. In his hand he bore the long spear of a minotaur beetle. He strutted, and looked scornfully down upon the whitely shining trap below him. He struck mushrooms, and they had fallen before him. He feared nothing. He strode fearlessly along. He would go to Saya and bring her to this land where food grew in abundance.

Sixty paces before him, a shaft sank vertically in the sandy, clayey soil. It was a carefully rounded shaft, and lined with silk. It went down for perhaps thirty feet or more, and there enlarged itself into a chamber where the owner and digger of the shaft might rest. The top of the hole was closed by a trap door, stained with mud and earth to imitate with precision the surrounding soil. A keen eye would have been needed to perceive the opening. But a keen eye now peered out from a tiny crack, the eye of the engineer of the underground dwelling.

Eight hairy legs surrounded the body of the creature that hung motionless at the top of the silk-lined shaft. A huge misshapen globe formed its body, colored a dirty brown. Two pairs of ferocious mandibles stretched before its fierce mouth-parts. Two eyes glittered evilly in the darkness of the burrow. And over the whole body spread a rough, mangy fur.

It was a thing of implacable malignance, of incredible ferocity. It was the brown hunting-spider, the American tarantula (*Mygale Hentzii*). Its body was two feet and more in diameter, and its legs, outstretched, would cover a circle three yards across. It watched Burl, its eyes glistening. Slaver welled up and dropped from its jaws.

And Burl strutted forward on the edge of the cliff, puffed up with a sense of his own importance. The white snare of the spinning spider below him impressed him as amusing. He knew the spider would not leave its web to attack him. He reached down and broke off a bit of fungus growing at his feet. Where he broke it, it was oozing a soupy liquid and was full of tiny maggots in a delirium of feasting. Burl flung it down into the web, and then laughed as the black bulk of the hidden spider swung down from its hiding place to investigate.

*

The tarantula, peering from its burrow, quivered with impatience. Burl drew near, and nearer. He was using his spear as a lever, now, and prying off bits of fungus to fall down the cliffside into the colossal web. The spider, below, went leisurely from one place to another, investigating each new missile with its palpi, then leaving them, as they appeared lifeless and undesirable prey. Burl laughed again as a particularly large lump of shelf-fungus narrowly missed the black-and-silver figure below. Then—

The trap door fell into place with a faint click, and Burl whirled about. His laughter turned to a scream. Moving toward him with incredible rapidity, the monster tarantula opened its dripping jaws. Its mandibles gaped wide. The poison fangs were unsheathed. The creature was thirty paces away, twenty paces—ten. It leaped into the air, eyes glittering, all its eight legs extended to seize, fangs bared—

Burl screamed again, and thrust out his arms to ward off the impact of the leap. In his terror, his grasp upon his spear had become agonized. The spear point shot out, and the tarantula fell upon it. Nearly a quarter of the spear entered the body of the ferocious thing.

It struck upon the spear, writhing horribly, still struggling to reach Burl, who was transfixed with horror. The mandibles clashed, strange sounds came from the beast. Then one of the attenuated, hairy legs rasped across Burl's forearm. He gasped in ultimate fear and stepped backward—and the edge of the cliff gave way beneath him.

He hurtled downward, still clutching the spear which led the writhing creature from him. Down through space, eyes glassy with panic, the two creatures—the man and the giant tarantula—fell together. There was a strangely elastic crash and crackling. They had fallen into the web beneath them.

Burl had reached the end of terror. He could be no more fear-struck. Struggling madly in the gummy coils of an immense web, which ever bound him more tightly, with a wounded creature shuddering in agony not a yard from him—yet a wounded creature that still strove to reach him with its poison fangs—Burl had reached the limit of panic.

He fought like a madman to break the coils about him. His arms and breast were greasy from the oily fish, and the sticky web did not adhere to them, but his legs and body were inextricably fastened by the elastic threads spread for just such prey as he.

He paused a moment, in exhaustion. Then he saw, five yards away, the silvery and black monster waiting patiently for him to weary himself. It judged the moment propitious. The tarantula and the man were one in its eyes, one struggling thing that had fallen opportunely into its snare. They were moving but feebly now. The spider advanced delicately, swinging its huge bulk nimbly along the web, paying out a cable after it came inexorably toward him.

Burl's arms were free, because of the greasy coating they had received. He waved them wildly, shrieking at the pitiless monster that approached. The spider paused. Those moving arms suggested mandibles that might wound or slap.

Spiders take few hazards. This spider was no exception to the rule. It drew cautiously near, then stopped. Its spinnerets became busy, and with one of its six legs, used like an arm, it flung a sheet of gummy silk impartially over both the tarantula and the man.

Burl fought against the descending shroud. He strove to thrust it away, but in vain. In a matter of minutes he was completely covered in a silken cloth that hid even the light from his eyes. He and his enemy, the giant tarantula, were beneath the same covering, though the tarantula moved but weakly.

The shower ceased. The web-spider had decided that they were helpless. Then Burl felt the cables of the web give slightly, as the spider approached to sting and suck the sweet juices from its prey.

THE MAD PLANET

*

The web yielded gently as the added weight of the black-bellied spider approached. Burl froze into stillness under his enveloping covering. Beneath the same silken shroud the tarantula writhed in agony upon the point of Burl's spear. It clashed its jaws, shuddering upon the horny barb.

Burl was quiet in an ecstasy of terror. He waited for the poison-fangs to be thrust into him. He knew the process. He had seen the leisurely fashion in which the giant spiders delicately stung their prey, then withdrew to wait without impatience for the poison to do its work.

When their victim had ceased to struggle, they drew near again, and sucked the sweet juices from the body, first from one point and then another, until what had so recently been a creature vibrant with life became a shrunken, withered husk—to be flung from the web at nightfall. Most spiders are tidy housekeepers, destroying their snares daily to spin anew.

The bloated, evil creature moved meditatively about the shining sheet of silk it had cast over the man and the giant tarantula when they fell from the cliff above. Now only the tarantula moved feebly. Its body was outlined by a bulge in the concealing shroud, throbbing faintly as it still struggled with the spear in its vitals. The irregularly rounded protuberance offered a point of attack for the web spider. It moved quickly forward, and stung.

Galvanized into fresh torment by this new agony, the tarantula writhed in a very hell of pain. Its legs, clustered about the spear still fastened into its body, struck out purposelessly, in horrible gestures of delirious suffering. Burl screamed as one of them touched him, and struggled himself.

His arms and head were free beneath the silken sheet because of the grease and oil that coated them. He clutched at the threads about him and strove to draw himself away from his deadly neighbor. The threads did not break, but they parted one from another, and a tiny opening appeared. One of the tarantula's attenuated limbs touched him again. With the strength of utter panic he hauled himself away, and the opening enlarged. Another struggle, and Burl's head emerged into the open air, and he stared down for twenty feet upon an open space almost carpeted with the chitinous remains of his present captor's former victims.

Burl's head was free, and his breast and arms. The fish slung over his shoulder had shed its oil upon him impartially. But the lower part of his body was held firm by the gummy snare of the web-spider, a snare far more tenacious than any bird-lime ever manufactured by man.

He hung in his tiny window for a moment, despairing. Then he saw, at a little distance, the bulk of the monster spider, waiting patiently for its poison to take effect and the struggling of its prey to be stilled. The tarantula was no more than shuddering now. Soon it would be still, and the black-bellied creature waiting on the web would approach for its meal.

Burl withdrew his head and thrust desperately at the sticky stuff about his loins and legs. The oil upon his hands kept it from clinging to them, and it gave a little. In a flash of inspiration, Burl understood. He reached over his shoulder and grasped the greasy fish; tore it in a dozen places and smeared himself with the now rancid exudation, pushing the sticky threads from his limbs and oiling the surface from which he had thrust it away.

He felt the web tremble. To the spider, its poison seemed to have failed of effect. Another sting seemed to be necessary. This time it would not insert its fangs into the quiescent tarantula, but would sting where the disturbance was manifest—would send its deadly venom into Burl.

He gasped, and drew himself toward his window. It was as if he would have pulled his legs from his body. His head emerged, his shoulders—half his body was out of the hole.

THE MAD PLANET

The colossal spider surveyed him, and made ready to cast more of its silken sheet upon him. The spinnerets became active, and the sticky stuff about Burl's feet gave way! He shot out of the opening and fell sprawling, awkwardly and heavily, upon the earth below, crashing upon the shrunken shell of a flying beetle which had fallen into the snare and had not escaped.

Burl rolled over and over, and then sat up. An angry, foot-long ant stood before him, its mandibles extended threateningly, while its antennae waved wildly in the air. A shrill stridulation filled the air.

In ages past, when ants were tiny creatures of lengths to be measured in fractions of an inch, learned scientists debated gravely if their tribe possessed a cry. They believed that certain grooves upon the body of the insects, after the fashion of those upon the great legs of the cricket, might offer the means of uttering an infinitely high-pitched sound too shrill for man's ears to catch.

Burl knew that the stridulation was caused by the doubtful insect before him, though he had never wondered how it was produced. The cry was used to summon others of its city, to help it in its difficulty or good fortune.

Clickings sounded fifty or sixty feet away. Comrades were coming to aid the pioneer. Harmless save when interfered with—all save the army ant, that is—the whole ant tribe was formidable when aroused. Utterly fearless, they could pull down a man and slay him as so many infuriated fox terriers might have done thirty thousand years before.

*

Burl fled, without debate, and nearly collided with one of the anchoring cables of the web from which he had barely escaped a moment before. He heard the shrill sound behind him suddenly subside. The ant, short-sighted as all ants were, no longer felt itself threatened and went peacefully about the business Burl had interrupted, that of finding among the gruesome relics beneath the spider's web some edible carrion which might feed the inhabitants of its city.

Burl sped on for a few hundred yards, and stopped. It behooved him to move carefully. He was in strange territory, and as even the most familiar territory was full of sudden and implacable dangers, unknown lands were doubly or trebly perilous.

Burl, too found difficulty in moving. The glutinous stuff from the spider's shroud of silk still stuck to his feet and picked up small objects as he went along. Old ant-gnawed fragments of insect armour pricked him even through his toughened soles.

He looked about cautiously and removed them, took a dozen steps and had to stop again. Burl's brain had been uncommonly stimulated of late. It had gotten him into at least one predicament—due to his invention of a spear—but had no less readily led to his escape from another. But for the reasoning that had led him to use the grease from the fish upon his shoulder in oiling his body when he struggled out of the spider's snare, he would now be furnishing a meal for that monster.

Cautiously, Burl looked all about him. He seemed to be safe. Then, quite deliberately, he sat down to think. It was the first time in his life that he had done such a thing. The people of his tribe were not given to meditation. But an idea had struck Burl with all the force of inspiration—an abstract idea.

When he was in difficulties, something within him seemed to suggest a way out. Would it suggest an inspiration now? He puzzled over the problem. Childlike—and savage-like—the instant the thought came to him, he proceeded to test it out. He fixed his gaze upon his foot. The sharp edges of pebbles, of the remains of insect-armour, of a dozen things, hurt his feet when he walked. They had done so ever since he had been born, but never had his feet been sticky so that the irritation continued with him for more than a single step.

Now he gazed upon his foot, and waited for the thought within him to develop. Meanwhile, he slowly removed the sharp-pointed fragments, one by one. Partly coated as they were with the half-liquid gum from his feet, they clung to his fingers as they had to his feet, except upon those portions where the oil was thick as before.

Burl's reasoning, before, was simple and of the primary order. Where oil covered him, the web did not. Therefore he would coat the rest of himself with oil. Had he been placed in the same predicament again, he would have used the same means of escape. But to apply a bit of knowledge gained in one predicament to another difficulty was something he had not yet done.

A dog may be taught that by pulling on the latchstring of a door he may open it, but the same dog coming to a high and close-barred gate with a latchstring attached, will never think of pulling on this second latchstring. He associates a latchstring with the opening of the door. The opening of a gate is another matter entirely.

Burl had been stirred to one invention by imminent peril. That is not extraordinary. But to reason in cold blood, as he presently did, that oil on his feet would nullify the glue upon his feet and enable him again to walk in comfort—that was a triumph. The inventions of savages are essentially matters of life and death, of food and safety. Comfort and luxury are only produced by intelligence of a high order.

Burl, in safety, had added to his comfort. That was truly a more important thing in his development than almost any other thing he could have done. He oiled his feet.

It was an almost infinitesimal problem, but Burl's struggles with the mental process of reasoning were actual. Thirty thousand years before him, a wise man had pointed out that education is simply training in thought, in efficient and effective thinking. Burl's tribe had been too much preoccupied with food and mere existence to think, and now Burl, sitting at the base of a squat toadstool that all but concealed him, reexemplified Rodin's "Thinker" for the first time in many generations.

For Burl to reason that oil upon the soles of his feet would guard him against sharp stones was as much a triumph of intellect as any masterpiece of art in the ages before him. Burl was learning how to think.

He stood up, walked, and crowed in sheer delight, then paused a moment in awe of his own intelligence. Thirty-five miles from his tribe, naked, unarmed, utterly ignorant of fire, of wood, of any weapons save a spear he had experimented with the day before, abysmally uninformed concerning the very existence of any art or science, Burl stopped to assure himself that he was very wonderful.

Pride came to him. He wished to display himself to Saya, these things upon his feet, and his spear. But his spear was gone.

*

With touching faith in the efficacy of this new pastime, Burl sat promptly down again and knitted his brows. Just as a superstitious person, once convinced that by appeal to a favorite talisman he will be guided aright, will inevitably apply to that talisman on all occasions, so Burl plumped himself down to think.

These questions were easily answered. Burl was naked. He would search out garments for himself. He was weaponless. He would find himself a spear. He was hungry—and would seek food, and he was far from his tribe, so he would go to them. Puerile reasoning, of course, but valuable, because it was consciously reasoning, consciously appealing to his mind for guidance in difficulty, deliberate progress from a mental desire to a mental resolution.

Even in the high civilization of ages before, few men had really used their brains. The great majority of people had depended upon machines and their leaders to think for them. Burl's tribefolk depended on their stomachs. Burl, however, was gradually developing the habit of thinking which makes for leadership and which would be invaluable to his little tribe.

He stood up again and faced upstream, moving slowly and cautiously, his eyes searching the ground before him keenly and his ears alert for the slightest sound of danger. Gigantic butterflies, riotous in coloring, fluttered overhead through the misty haze.

Sometimes a grasshopper hurtled through the air like a projectile, its transparent wings beating the air frantically. Now and then a wasp sped by, intent upon its hunting, or a bee droned heavily along, anxious and worried, striving in a nearly flowerless world to gather the pollen that would feed the hive.

Here and there Burl saw flies of various sorts, some no larger than his thumb, but others the size of his whole hand. They fed upon the juices that dripped from the maggot-infested mushrooms, when filth more to their liking was not at hand.

Very far away a shrill roaring sounded faintly. It was like a multitude of clickings blended into a single sound, but was so far away that it did not impress itself upon Burl's attention. He had all the strictly localized vision of a child. What was near was important, and what was distant could be ignored. Only the imminent required attention, and Burl was preoccupied.

Had he listened, he would have realized that army ants were abroad in countless millions, spreading themselves out in a broad array and eating all they came upon far more destructively than so many locusts.

Locusts in past ages had eaten all green things. There were only giant cabbages and a few such tenacious rank growths in the world that Burl knew. The locusts had vanished with civilization and knowledge and the greater part of mankind, but the army ants remained as an invincible enemy to men and insects, and the most of the fungus growths that covered the earth.

Burl did not notice the sound, however. He moved forward, briskly though cautiously, searching with his eyes for garments, food, and weapons. He confidently expected to find all of them within a short distance.

Surely enough he found a thicket—if one might call it so—of edible fungi no more than half a mile beyond the spot where he had improvised his sandals to protect the soles of his feet.

MURRAY LEINSTER

Without especial elation, Burl tugged at the largest until he had broken off a food supply for several days. He went on, eating as he did so, past a broad plain a mile and more across, being broken into odd little hillocks by gradually ripening and suddenly developing mushrooms with which he was unfamiliar.

The earth seemed to be in process of being pushed aside by rounded protuberances of which only the tips showed. Blood-red hemispheres seemed to be forcing aside the earth so they might reach the outer air.

Burl looked at them curiously, and passed among them without touching them. They were strange, and to him most strange things meant danger. In any event, he was full of a new purpose now. He wished garments and weapons.

Above the plain a wasp hovered, a heavy object dangling beneath its black belly, ornamented by a single red band. It was a wasp—the hairy sand-wasp—and it was bringing a paralyzed gray caterpillar to its burrow.

Burl watched it drop down with the speed and sureness of an arrow, pull aside a heavy, flat stone, and descend into the ground. It had a vertical shaft dug down for forty feet or more.

It descended, evidently inspected the interior, reappeared, and vanished into the hole again, dragging the gray worm after it. Burl, marching on over the broad plain that seemed stricken with some erupting disease from the number of red pimples making their appearance, did not know what passed below, but observed the wasp emerge again and busily scratch dirt and stones into the shaft until it was full.

The wasp had paralyzed a caterpillar, taken it to the already prepared burrow, laid an egg upon it, and rilled up the entrance. In course of time the egg would hatch into a grub barely as long as Burl's forefinger, which would then feed upon the torpid caterpillar until it had waxed large and fat. Then it would weave itself a chrysalis and sleep a long sleep, only to wake as a wasp and dig its way to the open air.

Burl reached the farther side of the plain and found himself threading the aisles of one of the fungus forests in which the growths were hideous, misshapen travesties upon the trees they had supplanted. Bloated, yellow limbs branched off from rounded, swollen trunks. Here and there a pear-shaped puff-ball, Burl's height and half as much again, waited craftily until a chance touch should cause it to shoot upward a curling puff of infinitely fine dust.

Burl went cautiously. There were dangers here, but he moved forward steadily, none the less. A great mass of edible mushroom was slung under one of his arms, and from time to time he broke off a fragment and ate of it, while his large eyes searched this way and that for threats of harm.

Behind him, a high, shrill roaring had grown slightly in volume and nearness, but was still too far away to impress Burl. The army ants were working havoc in the distance. By thousands and millions, myriads upon myriads, they were foraging the country, clambering upon every eminence, descending into every depression, their antennae waving restlessly and their mandibles forever threateningly extended. The ground was black with them, each was ten inches and more in length.

A single such creature would be formidable to an unarmed and naked man like Burl, whose wisest move would be flight, but in their thousands and millions they presented a menace from which no escape seemed possible. They were advancing steadily and rapidly, shrill stridulations and a multitude of clickings marking their movements.

The great helpless caterpillars upon the giant cabbages heard the sound of their coming, but were too stupid to flee. The black multitudes covered the rank vegetables, and tiny but voracious jaws began to tear at the flaccid masses of flesh.

MURRAY LEINSTER

Each creature had some futile means of struggling. The caterpillars strove to throw off their innumerable assailants by writhings and contortions, wholly ineffective. The bees fought their entrance to the gigantic hives with stings and wingbeats. The moths took to the air in helpless blindness when discovered by the relentless throngs of small black insects which reeked of formic acid and left the ground behind them denuded in every living thing.

Before the oncoming horde was a world of teeming life, where mushrooms and fungi fought with thinning numbers of giant cabbages for foothold. Behind the black multitude was—nothing. Mushrooms, cabbages, bees, wasps, crickets. Every creeping and crawling thing that did not get aloft before the black tide reached it was lost, torn to bits by tiny mandibles. Even the hunting spiders and tarantulas fell before the host of insects, having killed many in their final struggles, but overwhelmed by sheer numbers. And the wounded and dying army ants made food for their sound comrades.

There is no mercy among insects. Only the web-spiders sat unmoved and immovable in their colossal snares, secure in the knowledge that their gummy webs would discourage attempts at invasion along the slender supporting cables.

Surging onward, flowing like a monstrous, murky tide over the yellow, steaming earth, the army ants advanced. Their vanguard reached the river, and recoiled. Burl was perhaps five miles distant when they changed their course, communicating the altered line of march to those behind them in some mysterious fashion of transmitting intelligence.

Thirty thousand years before, scientists had debated gravely over the means of communication among ants. They had observed that a single ant finding a bit of booty too large for him to handle alone would return to the ant-city and return with others. From that one instance they deduced a language of gestures made with the antennae.

THE MAD PLANET

Burl had no wise theories. He merely knew facts, but he knew that the ants had some form of speech or transmission of ideas. Now, however, he was moving cautiously along toward the stamping grounds of his tribe, in complete ignorance of the black blanket of living creatures creeping over the ground toward him.

A million tragedies marked the progress of the insect army. There was a tiny colony of mining bees—Zebra bees—a single mother, some four feet long, had dug a huge gallery with some ten cells, in which she laid her eggs and fed her grubs with hard-gathered pollen. The grubs had waxed fat and large, became bees, and laid eggs in their turn, within the gallery their mother had dug out for them.

Ten such bulky insects now foraged busily for grubs within the ancestral home, while the founder of the colony had grown draggled and wingless with the passing of time. Unable to forage herself, the old bee became the guardian of the nest or hive, as is the custom among the mining bees. She closed the opening of the hive with her head, making a living barrier within the entrance, and withdrawing to give entrance and exit only to duly authenticated members of the extensive colony.

The ancient and draggled concierge of the underground dwelling was at her post when the wave of army ants swept over her. Tiny, evil-smelling feet trampled upon her. She emerged to fight with mandible and sting for the sanctity of the hive. In a moment she was a shaggy mass of biting ants, rending and tearing at her chitinous armour. The old bee fought madly, viciously, sounding a buzzing alarm to the colonists yet within the hive. They emerged, fighting as they came, for the gallery leading down was a dark flood of small insects.

*

For a few moments a battle such as would make an epic was in progress. Ten huge bees, each four to five feet long, fighting with legs and jaw, wing and mandible, with all the ferocity of as many tigers. The tiny, vicious ants covered them, snapping at their multiple eyes,

40

biting at the tender joints in their armour—sometimes releasing the larger prey to leap upon an injured comrade wounded by the huge creature they battled in common.

The fight, however, could have but one ending. Struggle as the bees might, herculean as their efforts might be, they were powerless against the incredible numbers of their assailants, who tore them into tiny fragments and devoured them. Before the last shred of the hive's defenders had vanished, the hive itself was gutted alike of the grubs it had contained and the food brought to the grubs by such weary effort of the mature bees.

The army ants went on. Only an empty gallery remained, that and a few fragments of tough armour, unappetizing even to the omniverous ants.

Burl was meditatively inspecting the scene of a recent tragedy, where rent and scraped fragments of a great beetle's shiny casing lay upon the ground. A greater beetle had come upon the first and slain him. Burl was looking upon the remains of the meal.

Three or four minims, little ants barely six inches long, foraged industriously among the bits. A new ant city was to be formed and the queen-ant lay hidden a half-mile away. These were the first hatchlings, who would feed the larger ants on whom would fall the great work of the ant-city. Burl ignored them, searching with his eyes for a spear or weapon.

Behind him the clicking roar, the high-pitched stridulations of the horde of army ants, rose in volume. Burl turned disgustedly away. The best he could find in the way of a weapon was a fiercely toothed hind leg. He picked it up, and an angry whine rose from the ground.

One of the black minims was working busily to detach a fragment of flesh from the joint of the leg, and Burl had snatched the morsel from him. The little creature was hardly half a foot in length, but it advanced upon Burl, shrilling angrily. He struck it with the leg and crushed it. Two of the other minims appeared, attracted by the noise the first had made. Discovering the crushed body of their fellow, they unceremoniously dismembered it and bore it away in triumph.

Burl went on, swinging the toothed limb in his hand. It made a fair club, and Burl was accustomed to use stones to crush the juicy legs of such giant crickets as his tribe sometimes came upon. He formed a half-defined idea of a club. The sharp teeth of the thing in his hand made him realize that a sidewise blow was better than a spearlike thrust.

The sound behind him had become a distant whispering, high-pitched, and growing nearer. The army ants swept over a mushroom forest, and the yellow, umbrella-like growths swarmed with black creatures devouring the substance on which they found a foothold.

A great bluebottle fly, shining with a metallic luster, reposed in an ecstasy of feasting, sipping through its long proboscis the dark-colored liquid that dripped slowly from a mushroom. Maggots filled the mushroom, and exuded a solvent pepsin that liquefied the white firm "meat."

They fed upon this soup, this gruel, and a surplus dripped to the ground below, where the bluebottle drank eagerly. Burl drew near, and struck. The fly collapsed into a writhing heap. Burl stood over it for an instant, pondering.

The army ants came nearer, down into a tiny valley, swarming into and through a little brook over which Burl had leaped. Ants can remain under water for a long time without drowning, so the small stream was but a minor obstacle, though the current of water swept many of them off their feet until they choked the brook-bed, and their comrades passed over their struggling bodies dry-shod. They were no more than temporarily annoyed, however, and presently crawled out to resume their march.

About a quarter of a mile to the left of Burl's line of march, and perhaps a mile behind the spot where he stood over the dead bluebottle fly, there was a stretch of an acre or more where the giant, rank cabbages had so far resisted the encroachments of the ever present mushrooms. The pale, cross-shaped flowers of the cabbages formed food for many bees, and the leaves fed numberless grubs and worms, and loud-voiced crickets which crouched about on the ground, munching busily at the succulent green stuff. The army ants swept into the green area, ceaselessly devouring all they came upon.

A terrific din arose. The crickets hurtled away in a rocketlike flight, in a dark cloud of wildly beating wings. They shot aimlessly in any direction, with the result that half, or more than half, fell in the midst of the black tide of devouring insects and were seized as they fell. They uttered terrible cries as they were being torn to bits. Horrible inhuman screams reached Burl's ears.

A single such cry of agony would not have attracted Burl's attention—he lived in the very atmosphere of tragedy—but the chorus of creatures in torment made him look up. This was no minor horror. Wholesale slaughter was going on. He peered anxiously in the direction of the sound.

A wild stretch of sickly yellow fungus, here and there interspersed with a squat toadstool or a splash of vivid color where one of the many "rusts" had found a foothold. To the left a group of awkward, misshapen fungoids clustered in silent mockery of a forest of trees. There a mass of faded green, where the giant cabbages stood.

With the true sun never shining upon them save through a blanket of thick haze or heavy clouds, they were pallid things, but they were the only green things Burl had seen. Their nodding white flowers with four petals in the form of a cross glowed against the yellowish green leaves. But as Burl gazed toward them, the green became slowly black.

From where he stood, Burl could see two or three great grubs in lazy contentment, eating ceaselessly on the cabbages on which they rested. Suddenly first one and then the other began to jerk spasmodically. Burl saw that about each of them a tiny rim of black had clustered. Tiny black motes milled over the green surfaces of the cabbages. The grubs became black, the cabbages became black.

Horrible contortions of the writhing grubs told of the agonies they were enduring. Then a black wave appeared at the further edge of the stretch of the sickly yellow fungus, a glistening, living wave, that moved forward rapidly with the roar of clickings and a persistent overtone of shrill stridulations.

The hair rose upon Burl's head. He knew what this was! He knew all too well the meaning of that tide of shining bodies. With a gasp of terror, all his intellectual preoccupations forgotten, he turned and fled in ultimate panic. And the tide came slowly on after him.

*

He flung away the great mass of edible mushroom, but clung to his sharp-toothed club desperately, and darted through the tangled aisles of the little mushroom forest with a heedless disregard of the dangers that might await him there. Flies buzzed about him loudly, huge creatures, glittering with a metallic luster. Once he was struck upon the shoulder by the body of one of them, and his skin was torn by the swiftly vibrating wings of the insect, as long as Burl's hand.

Burl thrust it away and sped on. The oil with which he was partly covered had turned rancid, now, and the odor attracted them, connoisseurs of the fetid. They buzzed over his head, keeping pace even with his headlong flight.

A heavy weight settled upon his head, and in a moment was doubled. Two of the creatures had dropped upon his oily hair, to sip the rancid oil through their disgusting proboscises. Burl shook them off with his hand and ran madly on. His ears were keenly attuned to the sound of the army ants behind him, and it grew but little farther away.

The clicking roar continued, but began to be overshadowed by the buzzing of the flies. In Burl's time the flies had no great heaps of putrid matter in which to lay their eggs. The ants—busy scavengers—carted away the debris of the multitudinous tragedies of the insect world long before it could acquire the gamey flavor beloved by the fly maggots. Only in isolated spots were the flies really numerous, but there they clustered in clouds that darkened the sky.

Such a buzzing, whirling cloud surrounded the madly running figure of Burl. It seemed as though a miniature whirlwind kept pace with the little pink-skinned man, a whirlwind composed of winged bodies and multi-faceted eyes. He twirled his club before him, and almost every stroke was interrupted by an impact against a thinly armoured body which collapsed with a spurting of reddish liquid.

An agonizing pain as of a red-hot iron struck upon Burl's back. One of the stinging flies had thrust its sharp-tipped proboscis into Burl's flesh to suck the blood.

Burl uttered a cry and—ran full tilt into the thick stalk of a blackened and draggled toadstool. There was a curious crackling as of wet punk or brittle rotten wood. The toadstool collapsed upon itself with a strange splashing sound. Many flies had laid their eggs in the fungoid, and it was a teeming mass of corruption and ill-smelling liquid.

With the crash of the toadstool's "head" upon the ground, it fell into a dozen pieces, and the earth for yards around was spattered with a stinking liquid in which tiny, headless maggots twitched convulsively.

The buzzing of the flies took on a note of satisfaction, and they settled by hundreds about the edges of the ill-smelling pools, becoming lost in the ecstacy of feasting while Burl staggered to his feet and darted off again. This time he was but a minor attraction to the flies, and but one or two came near him. From every direction they were hurrying to the toadstool feast, to the banquet of horrible, liquefied fungus that lay spread upon the ground.

Burl ran on. He passed beneath the wide-spreading leaves of a giant cabbage. A great grasshopper crouched upon the ground, its tremendous jaws crunching the rank vegetation voraciously. Half a dozen great worms ate steadily from their resting-places among the leaves. One of them had slung itself beneath an overhanging leaf—which would have thatched a dozen homes for as many men—and was placidly anchoring itself in preparation for the spinning of a cocoon in which to sleep the sleep of metamorphosis.

A mile away, the great black tide of army ants was advancing relentlessly. The great cabbage, the huge grasshopper, and all the stupid caterpillars upon the wide leaves would soon be covered with the tiny biting insects. The cabbage would be reduced to a chewed and destroyed stump, the colossal, furry grubs would be torn into a myriad mouthfuls and devoured by the black army ants, and the grasshopper would strike out with terrific, unguided strength, crushing its assailants by blows of its powerful hind legs and bites of its great jaws. But it would die, making terrible sounds of torment as the vicious mandibles of the army ants found crevices in its armour.

The clicking roar of the ants' advance overshadowed all other sounds, now. Burl was running madly, breath coming in great gasps, his eyes wide with panic. Alone of all the world about him, he knew the danger behind. The insects he passed were going about their business with that terrifying efficiency found only in the insect world.

*

There is something strangely daunting in the actions of an insect. It moves so directly, with such uncanny precision, with such utter indifference to anything but the end in view. Cannibalism is a rule, almost without exception. The paralysis of prey, so it may remain alive and fresh—though in agony—for weeks on end, is a common practice. The eating piecemeal of still living victims is a matter of course.

Absolute mercilessness, utter callousness, incredible inhumanity beyond anything known in the animal world is the natural and commonplace practice of the insects. And these vast cruelties are performed by armoured, machine-like creatures with an abstraction and a routine air that suggests a horrible Nature behind them all.

Burl nearly stumbled upon a tragedy. He passed within a dozen yards of a space where a female dung-beetle was devouring the mate whose honeymoon had begun that same day and ended in that gruesome fashion. Hidden behind a clump of mushrooms, a great yellow-banded spider was coyly threatening a smaller male of her own species. He was discreetly ardent, but if he won the favor of the gruesome creature he was wooing, he would furnish an appetizing meal for her some time within twenty-four hours.

Burl's heart was pounding madly. The breath whistled in his nostrils—and behind him, the wave of army ants was drawing nearer. They came upon the feasting flies. Some took to the air and escaped, but others were too engrossed in their delicious meal. The twitching little maggots, stranded upon the earth by the scattering of their soupy broth, were torn in pieces. The flies who were seized vanished into tiny maws. The serried ranks of black insects went on.

The tiny clickings of their limbs, the perpetual challenges and cross-challenges of crossed antennae, the stridulations of the creatures, all combined to make a high-pitched but deafening din. Now and then another sound pierced the noises made by the ants themselves. A cricket, seized by a thousand tiny jaws, uttered cries of agony. The shrill note of the crickets had grown deeply bass with the increase in size of the organs that uttered it.

There was a strange contrast between the ground before the advancing horde and that immediately behind it. Before, a busy world, teeming with life. Butterflies floating overhead on lazy wings, grubs waxing fat and huge upon the giant cabbages, crickets eating, great spiders sitting quietly in their lairs waiting with invincible patience for prey to draw near their trap doors or fall into their webs, colossal beetles lumbering heavily through the mushroom forests, seeking food, making love in monstrous, tragic fashion.

And behind the wide belt of army ants—chaos. The edible mushrooms gone. The giant cabbages left as mere stumps of unappetizing pulp, the busy life of the insect world completely wiped out save for the flying creatures that fluttered helplessly over an utterly changed landscape. Here and there little bands of stragglers moved busily over the denuded earth, searching for some fragment of food that might conceivably have been overlooked by the main body.

Burl was putting forth his last ounce of strength. His limbs trembled, his breathing was agony, sweat stood out upon his forehead. He ran a little, naked man with the disjointed fragment of a huge insect's limb in his hand, running for his insignificant life, running as if his continued existence among the million tragedies of that single day were the purpose for which the whole of the universe had been created.

He sped across an open space a hundred yards across. A thicket of beautifully golden mushrooms (*Agaricus caesareus*) barred his way. Beyond the mushrooms a range of strangely colored hills began, purple and green and black and gold, melting into each other, branching off from each other, inextricably tangled.

They rose to a height of perhaps sixty or seventy feet, and above them a little grayish haze had gathered. There seemed to be a layer of tenuous vapor upon their surfaces, which slowly rose and coiled, and gathered into a tiny cloudlet above their tips.

The hills, themselves, were but masses of fungus, mushrooms and fungoids of every description, yeasts, "musts," and every form of fungus growth which had grown within itself and about itself until this great mass of strangely colored, spongy stuff had gathered in a mass that undulated unevenly across the level earth for miles.

Burl burst through the golden thicket and attacked the ascent. His feet sank into the spongy sides of the hillock. Panting, gasping, staggering from exhaustion, he made his way up the top. He plunged into a little valley on the farther side, up another slope. For perhaps ten minutes he forced himself on, then collapsed. He lay, unable to move further, in a little hollow, his sharp-toothed club still clasped in his hands. Above him, a bright yellow butterfly with a thirty-foot spread of wing, fluttered lightly.

He lay motionless, breathing in great gasps, his limbs stubbornly refusing to lift him.

MURRAY LEINSTER

*

The sound of the army ants continued to grow near. At last, above the crest of the last hillock he had surmounted, two tiny antennae appeared, then the black glistening head of an army ant, the forerunner of its horde. It moved deliberately forward, waving its antennae ceaselessly. It made its way toward Burl, tiny clickings coming from the movements of its limbs.

A little wisp of tenuous vapor swirled toward the ant, a wisp of the same vapor that had gathered above the whole range of hills as a thin, low cloud. It enveloped the insect—and the ant seemed to be attacked by a strange convulsion. Its legs moved aimlessly. It threw itself desperately about. If it had been an animal, Burl would have watched with wondering eyes while it coughed and gasped, but it was an insect breathing through air-holes in its abdomen. It writhed upon the spongy fungus growth across which it had been moving.

Burl, lying in an exhausted, panting heap upon the purple mass of fungus, was conscious of a strange sensation. His body felt strangely warm. He knew nothing of fire or the heat of the sun, and the only sensation of warmth he had ever known was that caused when the members of his tribe had huddled together in their hiding place when the damp chill of the night had touched their soft-skinned bodies. Then the heat of their breaths and their bodies had kept out the chill.

This heat that Burl now felt was a hotter, fiercer heat. He moved his body with a tremendous effort, and for a moment the fungus was cool and soft beneath him. Then, slowly, the sensation of heat began again, and increased until Burl's skin was red and inflamed from the irritation.

The thin and tenuous vapor, too, made Burl's lungs smart and his eyes water. He was breathing in great, choking gasps, but the period of rest—short as it was—had enabled him to rise and stagger on. He crawled painfully to the top of the slope, and looked back.

49

THE MAD PLANET

The hill-crest on which he stood was higher than any of those he had passed in his painful run, and he could see clearly the whole of the purple range. Where he was, he was near the farther edge of the range, which was here perhaps half a mile wide.

It was a ceaseless, undulating mass of hills and hollows, ridges and spurs, all of them colored, purple and brown and golden-yellow, deepest black and dingy white. And from the tips of most of the pointed hills little wisps of vapor rose up.

A thin, dark cloud had gathered overhead. Burl could look to the right and left, and see the hills fading into the distance, growing fainter as the haze above them seemed to grow thicker. He saw, too, the advancing cohorts of the army ants, creeping over the tangled mass of fungus growth. They seemed to be feeding as they went, upon the fungus that had gathered into these incredible monstrosities.

The hills were living. They were not upheavals of the ground, they were festering heaps of insanely growing, festering mushrooms and fungus. Upon most of them a purple mould had spread itself so that they seemed a range of purple hills, but here and there patches of other vivid colors showed, and there was a large hill whose whole side was a brilliant golden hue. Another had tiny bright red spots of a strange and malignant mushroom whose properties Burl did not know, scattered all over the purple with which it was covered.

Burl leaned heavily upon his club and watched dully. He could run no more. The army ants were spreading everywhere over the mass of fungus. They would reach him soon.

Far to the right the vapor thickened. A column of smoke arose. What Burl did not know and would never know was that far down in the interior of that compressed mass of fungus, slow oxidization had been going on. The temperature of the interior had been raised. In the darkness and the dampness deep down in the hills, spontaneous combustion had begun.

Just as the vast piles of coal the railroad companies of thirty thousand years before had gathered together sometimes began to burn

50

fiercely in their interiors, and just as the farmers' piles of damp straw suddenly burst into fierce flames from no cause, so these huge piles of tinder-like mushrooms had been burning slowly within themselves.

There had been no flames, because the surface remained intact and nearly air-tight. But when the army ants began to tear at the edible surfaces despite the heat they encountered, fresh air found its way to the smouldering masses of fungus. The slow combustion became rapid combustion. The dull heat became fierce flames. The slow trickle of thin smoke became a huge column of thick, choking, acrid stuff that set the army ants that breathed it into spasms of convulsive writhing.

From a dozen points the flames burst out. A dozen or more columns of blinding smoke rose to the heavens. A pall of fume-laden smoke gathered above the range of purple hills, while Burl watched apathetically. And the serried ranks of army ants marched on to the widening furnaces that awaited them.

They had recoiled from the river, because their instinct had warned them. Thirty thousand years without danger from fire, however, had let their racial fear of fire die out. They marched into the blazing orifices they had opened in the hills, snapping with their mandibles at the leaping flames, springing at the glowing tinder.

*

The blazing area widened, as the purple surface was undermined and fell in. Burl watched the phenomenon without comprehension and even without thankfulness. He stood, panting more and more slowly, breathing more and more easily, until the glow from the approaching flames reddened his skin and the acrid smoke made tears flow from his eyes.

Then he retreated slowly, leaning on his club and looking back. The black wave of the army ants was sweeping into the fire, sweeping into the incredible heat of that carbonized material burning with an open flame. At last there were only the little bodies of stragglers from the great ant-army, scurrying here and there over the ground their comrades had denuded of all living things. The bodies of the main army had vanished—burnt to crisp ashes in the furnace of the hills.

There had been agony in that flame, dreadful agony such as no man would like to dwell upon. The insane courage of the ants, attacking with their horny jaws the burning masses of fungus, rolling over and over with a flaming missile clutched in their mandibles, sounding their shrill war cry while cries of agony came from them—blinded, their antennae burnt off, their lidless eyes scorched by the licking flames, yet going madly forward on flaming feet to attack, ever attack this unknown and unknowable enemy.

Burl made his way slowly over the hills. Twice he saw small bodies of the army ants. They had passed between the widening surfaces their comrades had opened, and they were feeding voraciously upon the hills they trod on. Once Burl was spied, and a shrill war cry was sounded, but he moved on, and the ants were busily eating. A single ant rushed toward him. Burl brought down his club, and a writhing body remained to be eaten later by its comrades when they came upon it.

Again night fell. The skies grew red in the west, though the sun did not shine through the ever present cloud bank. Darkness spread across the sky. Utter blackness fell over the whole mad world, save where the luminous mushrooms shed their pale light upon the ground and fireflies the length of Burl's arm shed their fitful gleams upon an earth of fungus growths and monstrous insects.

Burl made his way across the range of mushroom hills, picking his path with his large blue eyes whose pupils expanded to great size. Slowly, from the sky, now a drop and then a drop, now a drop and then a drop, the nightly rain that would continue until daybreak began.

Burl found the ground hard beneath his feet. He listened keenly for sounds of danger. Something rustled heavily in a thicket of mushrooms a hundred yards away. There were sounds of preening, and of delicate feet placed lightly here and there upon the ground.

Then the throbbing beat of huge wings began suddenly, and a body took to the air.

A fierce, down-coming current of air smote Burl, and he looked upward in time to catch the outline of a huge body—a moth—as it passed above him. He turned to watch the line of its flight, and saw a strange glow in the sky behind him. The mushroom hills were still burning.

He crouched beneath a squat toadstool and waited for the dawn, his club held tightly in his hands, and his ears alert for any sound of danger. The slow-dropping, sodden rain kept on. It fell with irregular, drumlike beats upon the tough top of the toadstool under which he had taken refuge.

Slowly, slowly, the sodden rainfall continued. Drop by drop, all the night long, the warm pellets of liquid came from the sky. They boomed upon the hollow heads of the toadstools, and splashed into the steaming pools that lay festering all over the fungus-covered earth.

And all the night long the great fires grew and spread in the mass of already half-carbonized mushroom. The flare at the horizon grew brighter and nearer. Burl, naked and hiding beneath a huge mushroom, watched it grow near him with wide eyes, wondering what this thing was. He had never seen a flame before.

The overhanging clouds were brightened by the flames. Over a stretch at least a dozen miles in length and from half a mile to three miles across, seething furnaces sent columns of dense smoke up to the roof of clouds, luminous from the glow below them, and spreading out and forming an intermediate layer below the cloudbanks.

It was like the glow of all the many lights of a vast city thrown against the sky—but the last great city had moulded into fungus-covered rubbish thirty thousand years before. Like the flitting of airplanes above a populous city, too, was the flitting of fascinated creatures above the glow.

*

THE MAD PLANET

Moths and great flying beetles, gigantic gnats and midges grown huge with the passing of time, they fluttered and danced the dance of death above the flames. As the fire grew nearer to Burl, he could see them.

Colossal, delicately formed creatures swooped above the strange blaze. Moths with their riotously colored wings of thirty-foot spread beat the air with mighty strokes, and their huge eyes glowed like carbuncles as they stared with the frenzied gaze of intoxicated devotees into the glowing flames below them.

Burl saw a great peacock moth soaring above the burning mushroom hills. Its wings were all of forty feet across, and fluttered like gigantic sails as the moth gazed down at the flaming furnace below. The separate flames had united, now, and a single sheet of white-hot burning stuff spread across the country for miles, sending up its clouds of smoke, in which and through which the fascinated creatures flew.

Feathery antennae of the finest lace spread out before the head of the peacock moth, and its body was softest, richest velvet. A ring of snow-white down marked where its head began, and the red glow from below smote on the maroon of its body with a strange effect.

For one instant it was outlined clearly. Its eyes glowed more redly than any ruby's fire, and the great, delicate wings were poised in flight. Burl caught the flash of the flames upon two great iridescent spots upon the wide-spread wings. Shining purple and vivid red, the glow of opal and the sheen of pearl, all the glory of chalcedony and chrysoprase formed a single wonder in the red glare of burning fungus. White smoke compassed the great moth all about, dimming the radiance of its gorgeous dress.

Burl saw it dart straight into the thickest and brightest of the licking flames, flying madly, eagerly, into the searing, hellish heat as a willing, drunken sacrifice to the god of fire.

Monster flying beetles with their horny wing-cases stiffly stretched, blundered above the reeking, smoking pyre. In the red light from

54

before them they shone like burnished metal, and their clumsy bodies with the spurred and fierce-toothed limbs darted like so many grotesque meteors through the luminous haze of ascending smoke.

Burl saw strange collisions and still stranger meetings. Male and female flying creatures circled and spun in the glare, dancing their dance of love and death in the wild radiance from the funeral pyre of the purple hills. They mounted higher than Burl could see, drunk with the ecstasy of living, then descended to plunge headlong to death in the roaring fires beneath them.

From every side the creatures came. Moths of brightest yellow with soft and furry bodies palpitant with life flew madly into the column of light that reached to the overhanging clouds, then moths of deepest black with gruesome symbols upon their wings came swiftly to dance, like motes in a bath of sunlight, above the glow.

And Burl sat crouched beneath an overshadowing toadstool and watched. The perpetual, slow, sodden raindrops fell. A continual faint hissing penetrated the sound of the fire—the raindrops being turned to steam. The air was alive with flying things. From far away, Burl heard a strange, deep bass muttering. He did not know the cause, but there was a vast swamp, of the existence of which he was ignorant, some ten or fifteen miles away, and the chorus of insect-eating giant frogs reached his ears even at that distance.

The night wore on, while the flying creatures above the fire danced and died, their numbers ever recruited by fresh arrivals. Burl sat tensely still, his wide eyes watching everything, his mind groping for an explanation of what he saw. At last the sky grew dimly gray, then brighter, and day came on. The flames of the burning hills grew faint as the fire died down, and after a long time Burl crept from his hiding place and stood erect.

A hundred yards from where he was, a straight wall of smoke rose from the still smouldering fungus, and Burl could see it stretching for miles in either direction. He turned to continue on his way, and saw the remains of one of the tragedies of the night.

A huge moth had flown into the flames, been horribly scorched, and floundered out again. Had it been able to fly, it would have returned to its devouring deity, but now it lay immovable upon the ground, its antennae seared hopelessly, one beautiful, delicate wing burned in gaping holes, its eyes dimmed by flame and its exquisitely tapering limbs broken and crushed by the force with which it had struck the ground. It lay helpless upon the earth, only the stumps of its antennae moving restlessly, and its abdomen pulsating slowly as it drew pain-racked breaths.

Burl drew near and picked up a stone. He moved on presently, a velvet cloak cast over his shoulders, gleaming with all the colors of the rainbow. A gorgeous mass of soft, blue moth fur was about his middle, and he had bound upon his forehead two yard-long, golden fragments of the moth's magnificent antennae. He strode on, slowly, clad as no man had been clad in all the ages.

After a little he secured a spear and took up his journey to Saya, looking like a prince of Ind upon a bridal journey—though no mere prince ever wore such raiment in days of greatest glory.

*

For many long miles Burl threaded his way through a single forest of thin-stalked toadstools. They towered three-man-heights high, and all about their bases were streaks and splashes of the rusts and moulds that preyed upon them. Twice Burl came to open glades wherein open, bubbling pools of green slime festered in corruption, and once he hid himself fearfully as a monster scarabeus beetle lumbered within three yards of him, moving heavily onward with a clanking of limbs as of some mighty machine.

Burl saw the mighty armour and the inward-curving jaws of the creature, and envied him his weapons. The time was not yet come, however, when Burl would smile at the great insect and hunt him for the juicy flesh contained in those armoured limbs.

Burl was still a savage, still ignorant, still timid. His principal advance had been that whereas he had fled without reasoning, he now paused to see if he need flee. In his hands he bore a long, sharp-pointed chitinous spear. It had been the weapon of a huge, unnamed flying insect scorched to death in the burning of the purple hills, which had floundered out of the flames to die. Burl had worked for an hour before being able to detach the weapon he coveted. It was as long and longer than Burl himself.

He was a strange sight, moving slowly and cautiously through the shadowed lanes of the mushroom forest. A cloak of delicate velvet in which all the colors of the rainbow played in iridescent beauty hung from his shoulders. A mass of soft and beautiful moth fur was about his middle, and in the strip of sinew about his waist the fiercely toothed limb of a fighting beetle was thrust carelessly. He had bound to his forehead twin stalks of a great moth's feathery golden antennae.

Against the play of color that came from his borrowed plumage his pink skin showed in odd contrast. He looked like some proud knight walking slowly through the gardens of a goblin's castle. But he was still a fearful creature, no more than the monstrous creatures about him save in the possession of latent intelligence. He was weak—and therein lay his greatest promise. A hundred thousand years before him his ancestors had been forced by lack of claws and fangs to develop brains.

Burl was sunk as low as they had been, but he had to combat more horrifying enemies, more inexorable threatenings, and many times more crafty assailants. His ancestors had invented knives and spears and flying missiles. The creatures about Burl had knives and spears a thousand times more deadly than the weapons that had made his ancestors masters of the woods and forests.

Burl was in comparison vastly more weak than his forebears had been, and it was that weakness that in times to come would lead him and those who followed him to heights his ancestors had never known. But now—

THE MAD PLANET

He heard a discordant, deep bass bellow, coming from a spot not twenty yards away. In a flash of panic he darted behind a clump of mushrooms and hid himself, panting in sheer terror. He waited for an instant in frozen fear, motionless and tense. His wide, blue eyes were glassy.

The bellow came again, but this time with a querulous note. Burl heard a crashing and plunging as of some creature caught in a snare. A mushroom fell with a brittle snapping, and the spongy thud as it fell to the ground was followed by a tremendous commotion. Something was fighting desperately against something else, but Burl did not know what creature or creatures might be in combat.

He waited for a long time, and the noise gradually died away. Presently Burl's breath came more slowly, and his courage returned. He stole from his hiding place, and would have made away, but something held him back. Instead of creeping from the scene, he crept cautiously over toward the source of the noise.

He peered between two cream-colored toadstool stalks and saw the cause of the noise. A wide, funnel-shaped snare of silk was spread out before him, some twenty yards across and as many deep. The individual threads could be plainly seen, but in the mass it seemed a fabric of sheerest, finest texture. Held up by the tall mushrooms, it was anchored to the ground below, and drew away to a tiny point through which a hole gave on some yet unknown recess. And all the space of the wide snare was hung with threads, fine, twisted threads no more than half the thickness of Burl's finger.

This was the trap of a labyrinth spider. Not one of the interlacing threads was strong enough to hold the feeblest of prey, but the threads were there by thousands. A great cricket had become entangled in the maze of sticky lines. Its limbs thrashed out, smashing the snare-lines at every stroke, but at every stroke meeting and becoming entangled with a dozen more. It thrashed about mightily, emitting at intervals the horrible, deep bass cry that the chirping voice of the cricket had become with its increase in size.

Burl breathed more easily, and watched with a fascinated curiosity. Mere death—even tragic death—as among insects held no great interest for him. It was a matter of such common and matter-of-fact occurrence that he was not greatly stirred. But a spider and his prey was another matter.

There were few insects that deliberately sought man. Most insects have their allotted victims, and will touch no others, but spiders have a terrifying impartiality. One great beetle devouring another was a matter of indifference to Burl. A spider devouring some luckless insect was but an example of what might happen to him. He watched alertly, his gaze traveling from the enmeshed cricket to the strange orifice at the rear of the funnel-shaped snare.

The opening darkened. Two shining, glistening eyes had been watching from the rear of the funnel. It drew itself into a tunnel there, in which the spider had been waiting. Now it swung out lightly and came toward the cricket. It was a gray spider (*Agelena labyrinthica*), with twin black ribbons upon its thorax, next the head, and with two stripes of curiously speckled brown and white upon its abdomen. Burl saw, too, two curious appendages like a tail.

It came nimbly out of its tunnel-like hiding place and approached the cricket. The cricket was struggling only feebly now, and the cries it uttered were but feeble, because of the confining threads that fettered its limbs. Burl saw the spider throw itself upon the cricket and saw the final, convulsive shudder of the insect as the spider's fangs pierced its tough armour. The sting lasted a long time, and finally Burl saw that the spider was really feeding. All the succulent juices of the now dead cricket were being sucked from its body by the spider. It had stung the cricket upon the haunch, and presently it went to the other leg and drained that, too, by means of its powerful internal suction-pump. When the second haunch had been sucked dry, the spider pawed the lifeless creature for a few moments and left it.

Food was plentiful, and the spider could afford to be dainty in its feeding. The two choicest titbits had been consumed. The remainder could be discarded.

A sudden thought came to Burl and quite took his breath away. For a second his knees knocked together in self-induced panic. He watched the gray spider carefully with growing determination in his eyes. He, Burl, had killed a hunting-spider upon the red-clay cliff. True, the killing had been an accident, and had nearly cost him his own life a few minutes later in the web-spider's snare, but he had killed a spider, and of the most deadly kind.

Now, a great ambition was growing in Burl's heart. His tribe had always feared spiders too much to know much of their habits, but they knew one or two things. The most important was that the snare-spiders never left their lairs to hunt—never! Burl was about to make a daring application of that knowledge.

He drew back from the white and shining snare and crept softly to the rear. The fabric gathered itself into a point and then continued for some twenty feet as a tunnel, in which the spider waited while dreaming of its last meal and waiting for the next victim to become entangled in the labyrinth in front. Burl made his way to a point where the tunnel was no more than ten feet away, and waited.

Presently, through the interstices of the silk, he saw the gray bulk of the spider. It had left the exhausted body of the cricket, and returned to its resting place. It settled itself carefully upon the soft walls of the tunnel, with its shining eyes fixed upon the tortuous threads of its trap. Burl's hair was standing straight up upon his head from sheer fright, but he was the slave of an idea.

He drew near and poised his spear, his new and sharp spear, taken from the body of an unknown flying creature killed by the burning purple hills. Burl raised the spear and aimed its sharp and deadly point at the thick gray bulk he could see dimly through the threads of the tunnel. He thrust it home with all his strength—and ran away at the top of his speed, glassy-eyed from terror.

A long time later he ventured near again, his heart in his mouth, ready to flee at the slightest sound. All was still. Burl had missed the horrible convulsions of the wounded spider, had not heard the frightful gnashings of its fangs as it tore at the piercing weapon, had not seen the silken threads of the tunnel ripped as the spider—hurt to death—had struggled with insane strength to free itself.

He came back beneath the overshadowing toadstools, stepping quietly and cautiously, to find a great rent in the silken tunnel, to find the great gray bulk lifeless and still, half-fallen through the opening the spear had first made. A little puddle of evil-smelling liquid lay upon the ground below the body, and from time to time a droplet fell from the spear into the puddle with a curious splash.

Burl looked at what he had done, saw the dead body of the creature he had slain, saw the ferocious mandibles, and the keen and deadly fangs. The dead eyes of the creature still stared at him malignantly, and the hairy legs were still braced as if further to enlarge the gaping hole through which it had partly fallen.

Exultation filled Burl's heart. His tribe had been but furtive vermin for thousands of years, fleeing from the mighty insects, hiding from them, and if overtaken but waiting helplessly for death, screaming shrilly in terror.

He, Burl, had turned the tables. He had slain one of the enemies of his tribe. His breast expanded. Always his tribesmen went quietly and fearfully, making no sound. But a sudden, exultant yell burst from Burl's lips—the first hunting cry from the lips of a man in three hundred centuries!

*

The next second his pulse nearly stopped in sheer panic at having made such a noise. He listened fearfully, but there was no sound. He drew near his prey and carefully withdrew his spear. The viscid liquid made it slimy and slippery, and he had to wipe it dry against a leathery toadstool. Then Burl had to conquer his illogical fear again before daring to touch the creature he had slain.

THE MAD PLANET

He moved off presently, with the belly of the spider upon his back and two of the hairy legs over his shoulders. The other limbs of the monster hung limp, and trailed upon the ground. Burl was now a still more curious sight as a gayly colored object with a cloak shining in iridescent colors, the golden antennae of a great moth rising from his forehead, and the hideous bulk of a gray spider for a burden.

He moved through the thin-stalked mushroom forest, and, because of the thing he carried, all creatures fled before him. They did not fear man—their instinct was slow-moving—but during all the millions of years that insects have existed, there have existed spiders to prey upon them. So Burl moved on in solemn state, a brightly clad man bent beneath the weight of a huge and horrible monster.

He came upon a valley full of torn and blackened mushrooms. There was not a single yellow top among them. Every one had been infested with tiny maggots which had liquefied the tough meat of the mushroom and caused it to drip to the ground below. And all the liquid had gathered in a golden pool in the center of the small depression. Burl heard a loud humming and buzzing before he topped the rise that opened the valley for his inspection. He stopped a moment and looked down.

A golden-red lake, its center reflecting the hazy sky overhead. All about, blackened mushrooms, seeming to have been charred and burned by a fierce flame. A slow-flowing golden brooklet trickled slowly over a rocky ledge, into the larger pool. And all about the edges of the golden lake, in ranks and rows, by hundreds, thousands, and by millions, were ranged the green-gold, shining bodies of great flies.

They were small as compared with the other insects. They had increased in size but a fraction of the amount that the bees, for example, had increased; but it was due to an imperative necessity of their race.

The flesh-flies laid their eggs by hundreds in decaying carcases. The others laid their eggs by hundreds in the mushrooms. To feed the maggots that would hatch, a relatively great quantity of food was needed, therefore the flies must remain comparatively small, or the body of a single grasshopper, say, would furnish food for but two or three grubs instead of the hundreds it must support.

Burl stared down at the golden pool. Bluebottles, greenbottles, and all the flies of metallic luster were gathered at the Lucullan feast of corruption. Their buzzing as they darted above the odorous pool of golden liquid made the sound Burl had heard. Their bodies flashed and glittered as they darted back and forth, seeking a place to alight and join in the orgy.

Those which clustered about the banks of the pool were still as if carved from metal. Their huge, red eyes glowed, and their bodies shone with an obscene fatness. Flies are the most disgusting of all insects. Burl watched them a moment, watched the interlacing streams of light as they buzzed eagerly above the pool, seeking a place at the festive board.

A drumming roar sounded in the air. A golden speck appeared in the sky, a slender, needle-like body with transparent, shining wings and two huge eyes. It grew nearer and became a dragonfly twenty feet and more in length, its body shimmering, purest gold. It poised itself above the pool and then darted down. Its jaws snapped viciously and repeatedly, and at each snapping the glittering body of a fly vanished.

A second dragonfly appeared, its body a vivid purple, and a third. They swooped and rushed above the golden pool, snapping in mid air, turning their abrupt, angular turns, creatures of incredible ferocity and beauty. At the moment they were nothing more or less than slaughtering-machines. They darted here and there, their many-faceted eyes burning with blood-lust. In that mass of buzzing flies even the most voracious appetite must be sated, but the dragonflies kept on. Beautiful, slender, graceful creatures, they dashed here and there above the pond like avenging fiends or the mythical dragons for which they had been named.

*

THE MAD PLANET

Only a few miles farther on Burl came upon a familiar landmark. He knew it well, but from a safe distance as always. A mass of rock had heaved itself up from the nearly level plain over which he was traveling, and formed an outjutting cliff. At one point the rock overhung a sheer drop, making an inverted ledge—a roof over nothingness—which had been pre-empted by a hairy creature and made into a fairylike dwelling. A white hemisphere clung tenaciously to the rock above, and long cables anchored it firmly.

Burl knew the place as one to be fearfully avoided. A Clotho spider (*Clotho Durandi, LATR*) had built itself a nest there, from which it emerged to hunt the unwary. Within that half-globe there was a monster, resting upon a cushion of softest silk. But if one went too near, one of the little inverted arches, seemingly firmly closed by a wall of silk, would open and a creature out of a dream of hell emerge, to run with fiendish agility toward its prey.

Surely, Burl knew the place. Hung upon the outer walls of the silken palace were stones and tiny boulders, discarded fragments of former meals, and the gutted armour from limbs of ancient prey. But what caused Burl to know the place most surely and most terribly was another decoration that dangled from the castle of this insect ogre. This was the shrunken, desiccated figure of a man, all its juices extracted and the life gone.

The death of that man had saved Burl's life two years before. They had been together, seeking a new source of edible mushrooms for food. The Clotho spider was a hunter, not a spinner of snares. It sprang suddenly from behind a great puff-ball, and the two men froze in terror. Then it came swiftly forward and deliberately chose its victim. Burl had escaped when the other man was seized. Now he looked meditatively at the hiding place of his ancient enemy. Some day—

But now he passed on. He went past the thicket in which the great moths hid during the day, and past the pool—a turgid thing of slime and yeast—in which a monster water snake lurked. He penetrated the little wood of the shining mushrooms that gave out light at night, and the shadowed place where the truffle-hunting beetles went chirping thunderously during the dark hours.

And then he saw Saya. He caught a flash of pink skin vanishing behind the thick stalk of a squat toadstool, and ran forward, calling her name. She appeared, and saw the figure with the horrible bulk of the spider upon its back. She cried out in horror, and Burl understood. He let his burden fall and then went swiftly toward her.

They met. Saya waited timidly until she saw who this man was, and then astonishment went over her face. Gorgeously attired, in an iridescent cloak from the whole wing of a great moth, with a strip of softest fur from a night-flying creature about his middle, with golden, feathery antennae bound upon his forehead, and a fierce spear in his hands—this was not the Burl she had known.

But then he moved slowly toward her, filled with a fierce delight at seeing her again, thrilling with joy at the slender gracefulness of her form and the dark richness of her tangled hair. He held out his hands and touched her shyly. Then, manlike, he began to babble excitedly of the things that had happened to him, and dragged her toward his great victim, the gray-bellied spider.

Saya trembled when she saw the furry bulk lying upon the ground, and would have fled when Burl advanced and took it upon his back. Then something of the pride that filled him came vicariously to her. She smiled a flashing smile, and Burl stopped short in his excited explanation. He was suddenly tongue-tied. His eyes became pleading and soft. He laid the huge spider at her feet and spread out his hands imploringly.

Thirty thousand years of savagery had not lessened the femininity in Saya. She became aware that Burl was her slave, that these wonderful things he wore and had done were as nothing if she did not approve. She drew away—saw the misery in Burl's face—and abruptly ran into his arms and clung to him, laughing happily. And quite suddenly Burl saw with extreme clarity that all these things he had done, even the slaying of a great spider, were of no importance whatever beside this most wonderful thing that had just happened, and told Saya so quite humbly, but holding her very close to him as he did so.

And so Burl came back to his tribe. He had left it nearly naked, with but a wisp of moth-wing twisted about his middle, a timid, fearful, trembling creature. He returned in triumph, walking slowly and fearlessly down a broad lane of golden mushrooms toward the hiding place of his people.

Upon his shoulders was draped a great and many-colored cloak made from the whole of a moth's wing. Soft fur was about his middle. A spear was in his hand and a fierce club at his waist. He and Saya bore between them the dead body of a huge spider—aforetime the dread of the pink-skinned, naked men. But to Burl the most important thing of all was that Saya walked beside him openly, acknowledging him before all the tribe.

www.ingramcontent.com/pod-product-compliance
Lightning Source LLC
Chambersburg PA
CBHW050905120626
46554CB00003B/1019